For Cheng-Shin and Paw;
  Lucy and Deirdre.

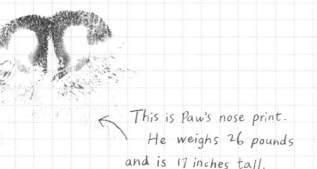

← This is Paw's nose print.
    He weighs 26 pounds
  and is 17 inches tall.

First U.S. edition 2004

Library of Congress Cataloging-in-Publication Data

Lee, Chinlun.
Good dog, Paw! / Chinlun Lee.
p.   cm.
Summary: When April the veterinarian treats animals in her office,
her well-loved dog, Paw, helps her and lets her patients know
the secret to good health.
ISBN 0-7636-2178-1
[1. Veterinarians–Fiction. 2. Dogs–Fiction. 3. Love–Fiction. 4. Animals–Fiction.] I. Title.
PZ7.L51188 Go 2004
[E]–dc21   2003048502

10 9 8 7 6 5 4 3 2 1

Printed in China

This book was typeset in Avenir Book.
The illustrations were done in watercolor and colored pencil.

Candlewick Press
2067 Massachusetts Avenue
Cambridge, Massachusetts 02140

visit us at www.candlewick.com

GOOD DOG, PAW!

Chinlun Lee

CANDLEWICK PRESS
CAMBRIDGE, MASSACHUSETTS

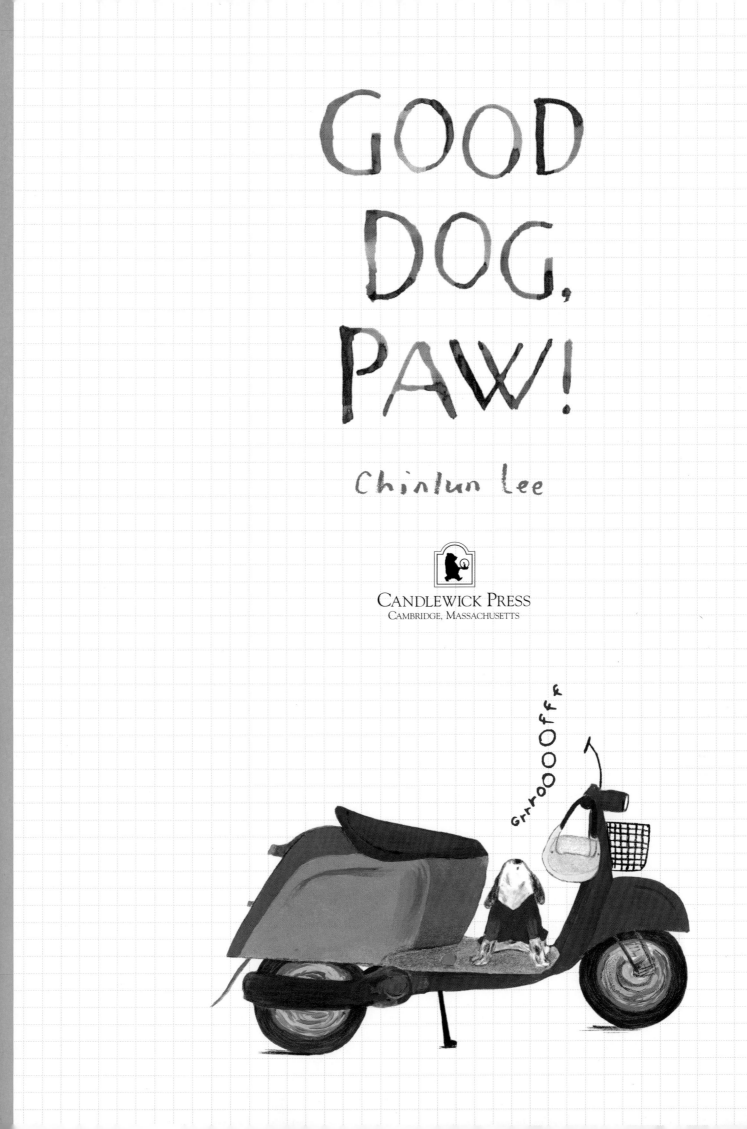

GrrrooOOFff

I am Paw.

This is April.

She's my owner.
She's a vet.

Having a vet for an owner is good.
Every morning I have a ten-point checkup
to see if I am healthy all over.

April says,

"ONE, your eyes, so bright!

TWO, your ears, so clean! No mites in sight!

THREE, your nose, so shiny!

FOUR, your breath, so fresh! So healthy!

FIVE,
your teeth,
so strong!

SIX,
your paws,
what pads,
what claws!

SEVEN,
your coat,
so warm and furry!

EIGHT,
your tummy,
so soft and
cuddly!

NINE, your tail,
so waggly!

TEN,
the whole of you,
so lovable!

Good dog,
Paw!"

After my checkup,
April does her exercises and I sing a song.

"I am Paw. I love April.
April loves me. I am Paw."

Then we get ready

and scoot away
to the clinic.

Please wait—
the vet is busy!

All day, April is
busy, busy, busy.
I sit in my chair and
sing soothing songs to
the animals waiting
to see her.

Poor Jackson the rabbit!

His teeth have grown out of his mouth.

I sing:

"Don't forget to eat your carrots, Jackson.

Carrots, carrots, carrots

keep your teeth short."

My big friend,
Salami the basset hound,
has a swollen tummy.

    I sing:

"Two pills a day will chase
those worms away!"

*sniff
sniff*

Silver the cat
is bristling with fleas.

I sing:

"My April will dust you,
dust you, dust you with
superstrength flea powder!"

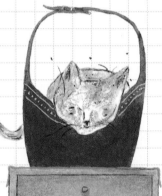

GRrrrroooooo^uuu

Old Sweet Pea the tortoise
cannot see well.

I sing:

"Don't be afraid, Sweet Pea!
A course of vitamins B, C, and A
will soon help you see again!"

wwWOOORrrrrooo

My animal friends like my songs.
They say I know a lot.

twitch
twitch

Woof!

But I only know what
April has taught me . . .

meow

and the best thing
she's taught me is this:

"Love. Love. Love.
Love. Love. Love.
The secret of health
is love."

At the end
of the day
April and I
say goodbye to
our last patients.

We play some games

and go to
the park
for a walk

and a slide.

Woof!
Woof!

Then we scoot home

and have dinner.

After dinner we sit together and April
gives me a ten-point checkup again.

She says,

"ONE,
your eyes,
so bright!

TWO,
your ears, so clean!
No mites
in sight!

THREE,

your nose,

so shiny!

FOUR, your breath,

so fresh! So healthy!

FIVE, your teeth, so strong!

SIX, your paws, what pads, what claws!

SEVEN, your coat,

so warm and furry!

EIGHT,

your tummy,

so soft and

cuddly!

NINE,
your tail,
so waggly!

TEN,
the whole of you,
so lovable!
Good dog,
Paw!"

April gets ready for bed
and I sing softly to her.
"April, my only April,
how I love you!"

April smiles.

"Good dog, Paw."